Samuel French Acting Edition

House Rules

by A. Rey Pamatmat

I0591595

‖SAMUEL FRENCH‖

SAMUELFRENCH.COM   SAMUELFRENCH.CO.UK

FOR PRODUCTION ENQUIRIES

UNITED STATES AND CANADA
Info@SamuelFrench.com
1-866-598-8449

UNITED KINGDOM AND EUROPE
Plays@SamuelFrench.co.uk
020-7255-4302

Each title is subject to availability from Samuel French, depending upon country of performance. Please be aware that *HOUSE RULES* may not be licensed by Samuel French in your territory. Professional and amateur producers should contact the nearest Samuel French office or licensing partner to verify availability.

MUSIC USE NOTE

Licensees are solely responsible for obtaining formal written permission from copyright owners to use copyrighted music in the performance of this play and are strongly cautioned to do so. If no such permission is obtained by the licensee, then the licensee must use only original music that the licensee owns and controls. Licensees are solely responsible and liable for all music clearances and shall indemnify the copyright owners of the play(s) and their licensing agent, Samuel French, against any costs, expenses, losses and liabilities arising from the use of music by licensees. Please contact the appropriate music licensing authority in your territory for the rights to any incidental music.

IMPORTANT BILLING AND CREDIT REQUIREMENTS

If you have obtained performance rights to this title, please refer to your licensing agreement for important billing and credit requirements.

HOUSE RULES was first produced by the Ma-Yi Theatre Company. The performance was directed by Ralph B. Peña, with scenic design by Reid Thompson, costume design by Martin Schnellinger, lighting design by Oliver Wason, and sound design by Fabian Obispo. The Production Stage Manager was Jennifer Delac. The cast was as follows:

ERNIE	Jojo Gonzalez
ROD	James Yaegashi
HENRY	Conrad Schott
JJ	Jeffrey Omura
MOMO	Tiffany Villarin
TWEE	Tina Chilip
VERA	Mia Katigbak

CHARACTERS

(in order of appearance)

ERNIE – late sixties, Filipino, Rod's and JJ's father

ROD – early thirties, Filipino-American, Ernie's oldest son

HENRY – early thirties, not Filipino, Rod's (recently ex-)boyfriend

JJ – late twenties, Filipino-American, Ernie's youngest son

MOMO – early thirties, Filipino-American, Vera's youngest daughter

TWEE – mid-thirties, Filipino-American, Vera's oldest daughter

VERA – sixties, Filipina, Twee's and Momo's mother

PLACE

New York City

TIME

Now

AUTHOR'S NOTE

For dialogue in Tagalog, translations are provided in brackets ("[" and "]"). The English translation is not meant to be spoken. Translations in quotations are meant to be spoken (see Scene Thirteen).

A "\" in dialogue indicates the place where the current character's line is interrupted by the subsequent character's line.

PROLOGUE

(Setting up.)

(Lights up on **ERNIE** *standing center with his hands folded in prayer. He's in church. Perhaps we hear a droned blessing from an offstage priest.)*

*(***ERNIE*** looks up. His gaze wanders as his focus drifts from the prayer. He sees a good-looking woman [in the audience?] and winks at her.)*

(A hymn begins as a flirtatious smile spreads across **ERNIE**'s *face. The smile stretches wider and wider, becomes more and more crooked. It twists into a wince.)*

*(***ERNIE**'s *breathing becomes quick, short, and shallow. His hand flies up and grabs his chest. He starts to jerk and make grunting noises, gripping onto the church pew in front of him.)*

Just as the hymn achieves ecstatic heights, **ERNIE** *squeals loudly, terrified. The organist fumbles and the music stops, as* **ERNIE** *falls onto the floor in front of his pew.)*

(Lights shift.)

(Player #1.)

(On another part of the stage, **ROD** *and* **HENRY** *in their apartment.)*

ROD. My family doesn't do small.

HENRY. Half of them are an ocean away.

ROD. They'll fly over for it.

HENRY. A gay wedding?

ROD. It's an excuse to gorge themselves on fancy food, get drunk, and sing karaoke.

HENRY. No karaoke.

ROD. No karaoke, no wedding.

HENRY. No wedding, no honeymoon.

ROD. No honeymoon, no…

HENRY. OKAY. Karaoke.

ROD. Okay.

HENRY. Okay, okay, okay.

> (**ROD** *and* **HENRY** *make out. Just as things are getting good, a cell phone rings. They break apart and sigh.*)

ROD. I'm on call.

HENRY. Me, too.

> (*They look at their phones.*)

Not me. The hospital?

ROD. No, Vera from upstairs. Let me just be sure…

> (**ROD** *answers the phone.*)

Hi. It's Toto.

Slow down.

No. Slow down.

My dad what?

> (*Lights shift.*)
>
> (*Player #2.*)
>
> (**JJ**, *alone in his home office, holding a sketchbook.*)
>
> (*He rips a page from the book and sets it on the floor. He rips out a second page and puts it next to the first. He rips out a third page and puts it on top of the first. He rips out a fourth page and puts it next to the second, making a new pile. He rips out a fifth and puts it with the fourth [on the new pile]. He rips and sorts pages quickly.*)
>
> (*Rips. Pile. Rips, pile, rips, pile…*)
>
> (*Faster and faster.*)

(There's a logic to the system, but we'll never figure out what it is. Even if we get close, we're interrupted, as…)

(JJ's phone rings.)

JJ. *(Answering.)* Hello?
What?

(Twenty seconds.)

I'll get on a plane.
No I can come now. I'll explain later. I'll be there soon.

(JJ hangs up. He takes a deep breath… And then he furiously rips page after page after page out of the sketchbook, crumpling them, tearing them up, eventually destroying the sketchbook.)

(Lights shift.)

*(**MOMO** with her sister **TWEE** in the living room of their mother's apartment.)*

(Player #3.)

MOMO. They just gave you money?

(Player #4.)

TWEE. A grant in recognition of future promise in the field of photography.

MOMO. What are you going to do with it?

TWEE. I'm going to "do" photography, and pay my rent for six months.

MOMO. Then what?

TWEE. Momo, not everyone goes high school, pre-med, med school, hospital, boring ass life of a total tool. Okay? Stop looking for linear progression in my career.

MOMO. I just don't get why you have to quit your job, just because you got this grant.

TWEE. When, exactly, did you start giving a shit?

*(**VERA** enters.)*

VERA. Language.

TWEE. Really?

VERA. Why weren't you in church?

TWEE. I'm never in church.

VERA. Momo? Why weren't you in church?

MOMO. There was this brunch thing –

VERA. I needed you at church.

TWEE. You didn't need me at church.

VERA. TWEE, NOT NOW!

> (*Pause.*)

TWEE. What's wrong?

VERA. Ernie.

TWEE. Ernie…?

MOMO. Toto and JJ's father.

TWEE. I know who he is. What did he do now?

VERA. In church…out of nowhere. He…

> (**VERA** *taps her chest.* **MOMO** *wraps a comforting arm around her mother.* **TWEE** *turns away from them, upset.*)

MOMO. Twee?

> (**TWEE** *turns, stares at them, and then walks offstage.*)
>
> (*Lights shift.*)
>
> (*A hospital bed appears, which* **ERNIE** *climbs into. The only hymn playing is the beep of a heart monitor.*)
>
> (*The others gather around the bed [except* **TWEE***].* **ROD** *clutches* **HENRY**. **VERA** *holds* **MOMO**. **JJ** *stands off to the side, lamely clutching a "get well" card.*)
>
> (*Suddenly,* **HENRY** *disengages from* **ROD** *and exits. After a beat,* **ROD**, **VERA**, *and* **MOMO** *exit as well, leaving* **JJ** *staring at* **ERNIE** *from afar.*)

(JJ *approaches but can't get himself all the way to* **ERNIE** *'s bedside.*)

(*Ten seconds.*)

(JJ *throws the card down nearby and then leaves.*)

End of Prologue

Scene One

(Two months later.)

*(**MOMO** and **VERA** playing gin rummy in **VERA**'s living room. **VERA** laughs at her own hilarity throughout.)*

VERA. I walked right into the break room…

MOMO. Mom, please stop. Please.

VERA. This is the only life you get. Sometimes, Momo, you have to go right in –

MOMO. No, you don't.

VERA. You have to own the things that happen to you in life, boldly.

MOMO. I do.

VERA. Boldly?

MOMO. No, but I own them.

VERA. I walked right into the break room, stood in front of the other nurses and Dr. Modi, and I just let it out. Then I said: "There! I farted."

MOMO. Oh, Jesus.

VERA. "There! I farted."

MOMO. That wasn't bold; it was rude.

VERA. It took courage!

MOMO. No, it took complete disregard for social norms.

VERA. What was I supposed to do?

MOMO. Go to the bathroom!

VERA. Our lunches are short, and we had to plan the party.

MOMO. Then hold it.

VERA. You know I can't. The minute I sat down or crossed my legs or bent over…

*(**VERA** makes an atypical fart noise, like a whistle or a series of finger snaps or a nonsensical onomatopoeic word. Nothing like a raspberry – nothing even close.)*

MOMO. Mom.

VERA. It's better to just come into the room and...

    (Atypical fart noise.)

    "There! I farted."

MOMO. Just shut up about it.

    Can you teach me how to make palabok for this fundraiser?

VERA. You want to make pancit palabok, too?

MOMO. I want to cook everything you cook. Someone has to learn, and Twee can't even make fried rice.

VERA. Twee, Twee, Twee.

    *(**MOMO** plays a winning hand.)*

MOMO. Gin.

VERA. You tricked me.

MOMO. Nope.

VERA. What rules are we using?

MOMO. It's gin rummy, so gin rummy rules.

VERA. But I have a rainbow.

MOMO. We're not playing with rainbows.

VERA. I could have won last turn, if I played my rainbow.

MOMO. We're not playing rainbows, and you didn't play the hand anyway.

VERA. I'm just telling you I could have won.

MOMO. No, you couldn't have, but fine. Whatever.

VERA. Fine. Twenty-five points.

MOMO. You can keep the points if you do me a favor instead.

VERA. But the rule is, win with gin and you get twenty-five points. Are you changing the rules?

MOMO. Not really.

VERA. Then I want to play my rainbow.

MOMO. We were already past the point where you could say, "Can I play this rainbow?"

VERA. And we're past the point now where you could say we're playing for favors instead of points.

MOMO. No, we're AT that point.

VERA. No.

MOMO. Yes.

VERA. No!

MOMO. Fine.

>*(A beat.)*

VERA. What's the favor?

MOMO. Why even tell you? Twenty-five points.

VERA. Momo.

MOMO. Make Twee stay somewhere else.

>*(A beat.)*

VERA. Twenty-five points…

MOMO. Mom.

VERA. I'm not putting your sister on the street. Her grant ran out, you know.

MOMO. Then she should get another grant, or – here's an idea – a job?

VERA. Photography is her job.

MOMO. Living off you is her job.

>*(**VERA** clucks her tongue.)*

Twee depends on you to catch her when she falls.

VERA. I'll catch you, too.

MOMO. You don't have to catch me.

VERA. One day I might, so don't criticize your sister. Honestly, I don't know what you two will do when I finally get sick of your fighting and kick the bucket.

MOMO. Maybe if you let her fall she'll learn to stand on her own.

VERA. Or maybe she'll keep falling.

MOMO. Well, when you're gone, and she needs me instead of you, I'm going to tell her to take care of herself.

VERA. Hay naku. Then get your dad in here, because we have to change the will and give Twee more money.

(**VERA** *starts to shuffle the cards.*)

MOMO. What money? I've been paying your maintenance since Dad retired.

VERA. Because we're stealing from you, idiot. I won the lottery, and we have a house in Monaco that we keep secret so you don't bother us while we entertain Princess Caroline.

MOMO. Well, good. Give that house to Twee. She can slut around with the high rollers there to survive instead of leeching off of you.

(**VERA** *sets down the cards and stares at* **MOMO** *with the disappointment only a mother can direct toward her child.*)

VERA. *(Hands over her womb.)* I shot you out. I can put you back!

MOMO. Mom, that's gross. She hates me more than I hate her.

VERA. She doesn't understand you.

MOMO. And therefore she hates me. That's Twee logic.

VERA. When your dad and I are gone, she'll understand, and you will help her. And you'll want to help her, because she will help you. And that is that.

MOMO. Well then for her sake, you two better not die.

VERA. MONICA. That is that.

(**MOMO** *is silenced. She takes the cards from her mother, shuffles them one more time, and deals.*)

How's Ernie?

MOMO. I don't know, really. He's not one of my patients. I know he got a lot better and then sort of plateaued.

VERA. Is he still in the hospital?

MOMO. Yes. It's been two months. He's out of the ICU, though.

VERA. Poor man.

MOMO. You should visit him. He doesn't get many visitors.

VERA. What about his sons?

MOMO. Toto is there every day. I'm sure Ernie would be happy to see you.

VERA. Maybe next week. I don't like the nurses in your hospital, though. I come in and just want to correct them all the time. They're not very good nurses.

MOMO. Mom, come on.

VERA. Except Sheila. She should come to my hospital. She's a very good nurse.

MOMO. Yeah. She is.

VERA. I thought Sheila did orthopedics.

MOMO. She is – does.

VERA. Then how do you know how good she is? She works on neurology cases?

MOMO. People talk. And we're roommates. And Dr. Lo told me Sheila is…good. She told me. Dr. Lo.

VERA. Sometimes, Momo, you have to walk into a room and own things. Boldly.

MOMO. I…try.

>*(The jangle of keys.* **VERA** *puts away the cards, as* **TWEE** *strides in wearing a sari. She hauls an enormous suitcase into the room, throws it down, and declares [boldly]:)*

TWEE. Here I am!

VERA. Welcome home!

>*(***VERA*** *hugs her, and then…)*

What are you wearing?

TWEE. A sari.

VERA. You wore that on the subway?

TWEE. I took a cab.

VERA. I thought you were out of money?

TWEE. "Nice to see you, Twee. Don't you look lovely!"
"Hi, Mom. How are you?"

VERA. Get changed. We're going to a party.

TWEE. I just got home!

VERA. My home. And if I tell you you're going to a party while you're staying in my home, you're going.

TWEE. Um, JET LAG?

VERA. It will pass faster if you stay awake and go to bed at a normal time.

TWEE. "How are you, Twee? How was India?"

MOMO. How was India?

TWEE. Shut up.

VERA. Don't start. Momo and I are going to cook. Put your things in your room, put on real clothes, and then we're going. It's a fundraiser for people who can't pay their hospital bills.

TWEE. Are you serious?

VERA. Someone who needs funds shouldn't refuse to help at a fundraiser.

TWEE. Can I cook something, too?

VERA. Change first.

> (**VERA** *exits.*)

> (**MOMO** *and* **TWEE** *stare at each other.*)

TWEE. What are you cooking?

MOMO. Pancit.

TWEE. Bihon?

MOMO. Palabok.

TWEE. Is it a Flip party?

MOMO. No. Mixed. Need help with the bag?

TWEE. No.

> (**TWEE** *picks up her suitcase and exits.*)

MOMO. Nice to see you, Twee.

End of Scene

Scene Two

(ERNIE *convalescing in a hospital.* ROD *stands at the foot of his bed.*)

(ERNIE *plays pyramid solitaire throughout the scene.*)

ERNIE. My son is a useless piece of shit.

ROD. Let's try to stay on topic.

ERNIE. The topic is shit. I shit myself, and you want to re-attach that shitbag.

ROD. That's not how I would put it.

ERNIE. That's not how they put it when my son was born, but I shit myself one useless piece of shit.

ROD. If your hips are in such pain you'd prefer to soil yourself \ instead –

ERNIE. No one *prefers* to shit themselves.

ROD. If you prefer that over enduring soreness in your hips on the way to the toilet, then we should consider other arrangements for your comfort.

ERNIE. The shitbag.

ROD. The…yes.

ERNIE. Do you know what would make me comfortable? If you shot me in the goddamn face! Because when someone's options are: a) shitting themselves or b) taking ten excruciating steps to the commode, it's probably best to skip to euthanasia.

ROD. Will you please –?

ERNIE. KILL ME.

ROD. Current medical practice does not permit me to provide on demand suicides.

ERNIE. I'm not asking for suicide. I'm asking for murder. Kill me.

ROD. Assisted suicide.

ERNIE. I am, apparently, incapable of suicide. I would have preferred that blondie blonde nurse found me dead instead of reclining in a pool of my own soupy shit. But this body will not let go. A stroke, hip replacement, back surgery, emphysema, liver failure, and two heart attacks, and now, they tell me, diabetes. I would rather be dead.

ROD. Could you pause your rant while I dispense some medical advice? I have other patients.

    (**ERNIE** *flings a card at* **ROD.**)

ERNIE. Shoot.

ROD. Thank you –

    (Card.)

ERNIE. Fire away.

ROD. I would li –

    (Card.)

ERNIE. Shoot me IN THE GODDAMN FACE.

ROD. I will not shoot you in the face, hellbound though it may be. I will recommend the nurse re-attach –

ERNIE. Re-attach the shitbag.

ROD. So you won't hurt yourself on the way to the toilet. We'll give you a stronger painkiller to help you with your general discomfort, too.

ERNIE. If there was a nurse here all the time like on the other floor, I wouldn't have shit myself in the first place.

ROD. This isn't an intensive care floor. You're on the mend.

ERNIE. I shit myself! I want a nurse here all the time. That Russian one.

ROD. Romanian.

ERNIE. Whatever. Just no Americans. They're lazy and want to do the least work for the most money. They're just waiting for a man to marry them. I want that hardworking Romanian nurse with the impressive chest.

ROD. "Impressive chest"?

ERNIE. I bet that heifer shot out some strong, healthy kids – nothing like my piece of shit son. That Russian or

Romanian is a good woman. Most women just want to rob you blind. They clean your house and cook your meals and let you do whatever you want in the sack –

ROD. Oh, god.

ERNIE. Until you're married. Then the laundry piles up and you eat frozen pizzas every week and you're lucky if you have a free minute from her moaning to sneak off and take care of your own business.

ROD. Please don't talk about –

ERNIE. WHERE IS MY USELESS SON? WHY IS HE LEAVING ME HERE?! WHY ISN'T THAT USELESS PIECE OF SHIT HERE RIGHT NOW?

> *(Silence.)*
>
> *(**ERNIE** holds out a hand. **ROD** passes back the cards that were flung at him. **ERNIE** plays solitaire once again.)*

ROD. I'll bring JJ around next time, I promise.

ERNIE. JJ?

ROD. I'll make Johan visit.

ERNIE. Not JJ. Roderick. My doctor son who could have gotten me onto a floor with a twenty-four hour nurse if he weren't such a USELESS piece. Of. Shit.

> *(Silence.)*

ROD. Okay… I'll find out why your piece of shit doctor son hasn't come, I'll re-attach your shitbag, and I'll sedate the hell out of you, so you'll feel like you were shot in the goddamn face.

ERNIE. And the Russian with the tits.

ROD. …Fine…

> *(**ROD** steps away from the bed just as **HENRY** enters and intercepts him.)*

HENRY. Hey, Rod. How's your dad?

ROD. He's a loud, foul-mouthed, racist, misogynist curmudgeon.

HENRY. More himself than ever?

ROD. He didn't recognize me. He's experiencing some kind of dementia.

HENRY. Painkillers, maybe. You okay?

ROD. I'm under a lot of stress.

HENRY. Yeah.

I'm sorry.

ROD. Bullshit.

HENRY. Oh…no. I was expressing sympathy, for…

ROD. I know. But everything you say is bullshit.

HENRY. We should talk –

ROD. We have nothing to talk about.

HENRY. Your dad has been the same for days. With all the attention and care he's getting, the same isn't good. It's waiting for something bad to –

ROD. I'm also a fucking doctor, Henry.

HENRY. You're his son. Sometimes family members need to be reminded…

(*HENRY puts a hand on* **ROD**'s *shoulder.* **ROD** *pushes him off, roughly.*)

ROD. You have lost the privilege of showing me kindness. I would rather you shot me in the goddamn face. Admin called me this morning. What kind of epic headfuck are you playing at, asking to be my dad's doctor after what you did?

HENRY. I don't know. I'm not…

ROD. I have to keep my life together, my loser brother's life together, and a man alive who has told me several times he wished I was dead. I don't have time for your pathetic consolation prize of consolation.

I have rounds.

(**ROD** *exits.* **HENRY** *looks at* **ERNIE**'s *chart.*)

ERNIE. Henry, where's my son?

HENRY. He just left.

ERNIE. Why won't he help me?

HENRY. He's trying.

ERNIE. Is he angry with me?

HENRY. He's doing his best, given the…circumstances. We're all just trying to do our best.

> (**HENRY** *reaches out for the cards.* **ERNIE** *clutches them and rolls over.*)

End of Scene

Scene Three

(**TWEE** *and* **MOMO** *playing sungka in* **VERA**'s *living room.* **TWEE** *is winning.*)

MOMO. Are you cheating?

TWEE. Fuck you and your mother.

MOMO. Your mother, too.

TWEE. Don't remind me.

(**MOMO** *finally gets a turn but winds up dead after once around the board.*)

You suck at this.

MOMO. Shut up.

TWEE. You suck at everything. I mean that pancit palabok yesterday…

MOMO. It didn't suck.

(**TWEE** *starts a turn.*)

TWEE. Did anyone eat it? I didn't even eat it, and I like palabok. It was so embarrassing. Momo, white people don't eat shrimp heads.

MOMO. White people eat shrimp.

TWEE. They're white. They're already scared, because it's a foreign food, and this food is orange with squid rings and tentacles and slices of hard-boiled egg like weird yellow eyeballs.

MOMO. SHUT. UP.

TWEE. And then you throw in shrimp with the heads on?

MOMO. I peeled all of the shrimp, except for three.

TWEE. And you placed those right on top.

MOMO. I wanted it to be authentic.

TWEE. Mo, when white people say "authentic" they mean two steps better than fusion, but two steps less than real. Behead and shell all of the shrimp. Cut the squid entirely. Or bread slices of the body, fry them, and throw them on top.

MOMO. That's calamari.

TWEE. EXACTLY. Two better than fusion, two less than real. And next time write out a cute little sign that says, "Asian Rice Noodles with Shrimp!" Not Filipino, Asian. Maybe have a picture of a coconut tree.

MOMO. There's no coconut in palabok.

TWEE. The point is, no one wants to know what we REALLY eat: blood soup, fertilized unborn duck chicks still in the shell. You going to bring balut to the next potluck? It's sooooooo "authentic."

MOMO. Well, you brought Indian food. What the heck is that?

TWEE. Chicken tikka. I took a cooking class in Mumbai.

MOMO. That's not white people food.

TWEE. But they already know what it is.

MOMO. You're full of crap.

TWEE. Oh! Watch out everyone! Momo's breaking out the "LANGUAGE"! She said…

> *(Whispering.)*

…crap…!

> *(Normal voice.)*

I think she even said heck!

> *(By the way, we haven't forgotten;* **TWEE***'s turn is still going.)*

What's with this über-Filipino schtick anyway? It's like you suddenly forgot we were born and raised in the U. S. of A.

MOMO. To Filipino parents who won't be around forever. Mom and Dad will pass away eventually.

TWEE. So now you're the one who cooks the pancit?

Our parents were smart. They didn't teach us Tagalog, because they knew: you've got to assimilate to succeed here. You've got to be just exotic enough to be interesting but not so exotic you're alien.

Asian rice noodles with shrimp, not pancit palabok.

MOMO. Do you have to criticize everything I say?

TWEE. And do.

MOMO. The only reason you know so much about white people is because you took your little rich white girl trip to India, took a cooking class, did some yoga. Wow.

TWEE. Your precious mother loved my chicken.

MOMO. WHY HASN'T YOUR TURN ENDED?

> (Holy crap, **TWEE** is still going around and around the board.)

TWEE. No wonder you can't get a man.

Is this all part of some new strategy to walk up to guys and spout Tagalog? Go to a club, dance tinikling, and sing to a pandanggo? When you get him home, are you going to kneel by the bed and pray the rosary together?

> (With a heavy Filipino accent.)

Hail Mary,

Pull op graces,

Dhe Lord is with dhee.

Blessed art dhou amongst women,

And blessed is dhe pruit op dhy womb, Jesus!

> (Seductively.)

Put it in my womb, ha! Let's make a Jesus op our own, but screw dhis Birgin Birth shit – excuse me – STUFF!

> (**TWEE**'s turn finally ends across from the biggest house on the board. She tries to take the shells into her pot, but there are so many of them that they spill a bit. When she finally has every...last...one... **MOMO** stares at the board, dismayed. Suddenly, she picks it up, throws all the shells on **TWEE**, and brandishes it like a weapon.)

MOMO. WHAT KIND OF SISTER ARE YOU! "You suck! This game sucks! Everything you do sucks! Your hair looks stupid! That outfit is stupid! YOU'RE STUPID!" Well, you know what, Twee? YOU'RE STUPID! A STUPID PIECE OF CRAP! YES. CRAAAAAAAP.

Maybe some of us are fine looking au naturel. Some of us don't measure our self-esteem by whether or not our hair bounces like Beyoncé's. Some of us don't need to look like high fashion, call girl assassins who know how to put makeup on so we don't look like clowns or triple-threat actor/singer/dancers in *Cats.* Because I HATE your shoes, your stupid slut heels! And I HATE that you call them slut heels! And I HATE when you tell me I need a pair!

Because you're so mean! I don't want to look anything like a person who would be mean to her baby sister. My friends' older sisters looked out for them and taught them how to pick nice clothes and whatever. But I got you. YOU! You mean, horrible piece of crap crap crap crap crap crap CRAP!! YOU!!

And maybe I don't want one of those smelly, farting, unshowered, unshaven jerks that your slut heels attract praying for this sinner now and at the hour of her death. AMEN.

AAAAAAAMEEEEEEEN –

> (**TWEE** *rips the board from* **MOMO**'s *hands.* **MOMO** *freezes.*)

TWEE. I'm helping you.

Without me, you'd be such a pathetic soul that you would have killed yourself at fifteen.

I make you face reality.

White people do not eat shrimp with the head on.

No man wants a girl with that rat's nest you call hair.

Listen to me and learn to play the game or prepare for a motherfucking solitary existence, pinay. Because your soft mama's girl ass needs a spine, and don't give me shit for mixing metaphors, because I know asses don't have spines.

When our precious mother does kick the bucket, you're going to be so fucking happy I pushed you to stand up for yourself and live your life and grow an ass spine that you're going to drop down and kiss my smoking hot, slut-heeled feet.

> *(**TWEE** shoves the sungka board back into **MOMO**'s hands.)*

Go on. Hit me.

MOMO. I don't need your lessons. They're cynical and, frankly, sad.

> *(**MOMO** puts the board down.)*

TWEE. Whatever, Momo. I don't have time to fight you anyway. The boys will be here soon.

Clean up this mess. That'll make you more Filipino than me. Pretend you're a hotel maid.

> *(**TWEE** tosses her hair and struts out, leaving **MOMO** surrounded by sungka shells. **MOMO** sighs and starts to clean up the game.)*

End of Scene

Scene Four

(**ROD** *and* **JJ** *on their way to* **VERA**'s *[which is in the same building]. They exit* **ROD**'s *apartment, ride an elevator, walk down a hall, and stop in front of* **VERA**'s *and her husband's.*)

ROD. You are a useless piece of shit.

JJ. Thanks, Toto.

ROD. Rod.

JJ. Right. Do I really have to call you Rod?

ROD. I'm done with the nicknames.

JJ. What's wrong with Toto? Because I can tell you with a change in vocal inflection and an arched eyebrow what's wrong with Rod.

ROD. Toto is a dog's name.

JJ. Rod is a penis's name.

ROD. It's short for Roderick, which is actually the name our mother gave me.

JJ. Our mother also gave you the name Toto when you were five and made up that dance routine to the *Africa* song.

ROD. Well we're grown men now, and my name is Rod.

(*Seeing* **JJ**'s *clothes.*)

You couldn't even get dressed? Aren't those the clothes you wore this morning, which may, actually, also be the ones you wore last night?

JJ. I was not wearing these clothes last night. The pants, but they're pants. And the shoes, but these are my most comfortable shoes. All the stuff that counts, though, is clean and fresh as of this morning. Besides, it's just game night.

ROD. A game night party.

JJ. And I distinctly recall you showing up to several of Momo and Twee's game nights in undergrad smelling like bong water.

ROD. I never smelled like –

JJ. You did.

ROD. No, I –

JJ. YOU. DID.

ROD. Well, this is the first game night in awhile, and I don't smell like bong water now. This isn't undergrad. You should be cleaned up for a party like an adult.

JJ. I didn't even want to come in the first place.

ROD. You don't even have to leave the building.

JJ. I don't want to leave the apartment.

ROD. You are not turning into Howard Hughes. Not on my couch. You lost your job. Fine. But if you're supposed to be some hot shot comic artist, why let this turn you into such a useless piece of shit?

> *(They're at* **VERA**'s *door [maybe they have been for awhile].* **ROD** *knocks.)*

JJ. Why are you knocking?

ROD. And visit Dad in the hospital.

> *(***JJ** *huffs and pushes open the door before anyone can answer.)*

> *(Lights shift as they enter the apartment.* **MOMO** *greets them.* **TWEE** *sits nearby, sipping whiskey.)*

MOMO. Hey!

JJ. Hi.

TWEE. Wassup, suckaaaas?

ROD. Hey, Mo.

MOMO. I need to talk to you.

> *(***MOMO** *tries to quickly pull* **ROD** *aside, but* **TWEE** *stops them.)*

TWEE. Momo fucked up. Henry's here.

JJ. Where?

TWEE. Bathroom now, but he is in the apartment.

> *(Smiling broadly.)*

Hi, Toto!

ROD. Twee.

TWEE. Mo. Fucked. Up.

MOMO. I was talking to Sheila, and he was just…lingering. I told her to come, if she could shift her schedule, and I guess he thought it was an open invitation.

ROD. No, he didn't. He took advantage.

MOMO. He wouldn't do that. He thought it was a PARTY party, not just game night.

JJ. JUST game night. See, Toto?

ROD. Shut up. ROD.

TWEE. Hell, I'm going to party. This is a party.

ROD. *(To* **MOMO.***)* Is Sheila here?

MOMO. No. Just us and Henry.

TWEE. Mo. Fucked. Up.

> (**HENRY** *enters with wet hands.*)

> *(Smiling broadly.)* Hi, Henry!

HENRY. Hi, again.

JJ. How are you, Henry? It's been awhile.

HENRY. Yeah. Yes, but –

JJ. Since…?

HENRY. Since, uh…

JJ. Since Dad's heart attack. You haven't been by Rod's since Dad's heart attack.

HENRY. Yes.

JJ. That's weird.

> *(Silence.)*

HENRY. Mo, there was no towel. No hand towel.

MOMO. Oh, sorry, I'll –

TWEE. No, no, no, no, no. You, Rod, and Henry stay right here. JJ will get one.

JJ. Excuse me?

TWEE. I want to watch.

JJ. Henry and I need to talk about where he's been since Dad's \ heart –

HENRY. I've been with Ernie in the hospital, JJ. I haven't been to Rod's, but I've been with him. Where have you \ been for the past –

JJ. I'll be right back.

> (JJ *exits for a towel.* **ROD** *shoots daggers at* **TWEE**, *and then walks up to* **HENRY**.)

ROD. Henry.

HENRY. Hey, how are you?

ROD. I saw you at work yesterday.

HENRY. I know, but how have you been since then?

ROD. This is awkward \ but –

HENRY. *(Too quickly.)* Mo invited me.

ROD. No, she didn't.

HENRY. She and Sheila \ were –

ROD. She didn't. It was a mistake. You should leave. Don't play dumb. Just leave.

HENRY. Can you – will you step outside with me?

ROD. No.

TWEE. Why not?

HENRY. Yeah. Why?

ROD. Twee, this is none of your business.

TWEE. Then step outside with him, where I can't hear you.

MOMO. Let's give them privacy.

TWEE. Rod doesn't want privacy, or he'd step outside.

HENRY. Look…let's talk alone.

ROD. If you wanted to talk to me alone, HENRY, YOU SHOULDN'T HAVE DUMPED ME.

HENRY. That's not a fair characterization of what happened \ and you –

ROD. GOODBYE.

MOMO. We'll see you at work tomorrow, okay?

> *(Five seconds.)*

HENRY. Okay.

(**HENRY** *goes. As he does.*)

TWEE. Thanks for stopping by, Hank! It was a pleasure! Have a good night! Get home safe, bon voyage, and bonne journée!

> (**JJ** *re-enters with a towel, sees that* **HENRY** *has already gone, and throws it at* **TWEE.**)

Watch it, slugger.

ROD. *(To* **TWEE.**) What the hell was that?

TWEE. I kept you from having to be alone with him. I was helping.

ROD. That was not helping.

TWEE. It was, and now I deserve to know: why don't you want to be alone with him?

MOMO. *(To* **TWEE.**) What are you doing?

TWEE. It's game night. I'm playing games!

> (**VERA** *enters with mahjong.*)

VERA. We don't have to play.

TWEE. Mooooooom.

VERA. I just said we don't have to play. Play whatever game you want, and if at some point you want to love the woman who labored to bring you into this beautiful, beautiful world, then I can teach you mahjong.

TWEE. Monopoly.

MOMO. Finally something we can agree on.

> (*They start setting up the game.*)

VERA. But it takes forever.

TWEE. You got some place to be, woman?

VERA. Twee.

TWEE. I mean, dearest Mommy, darling, dear?

ROD. I'm the car.

TWEE. Whoa, whoa, whoa...

MOMO. Iron. I'll be banker.

ROD. *(To* **TWEE**.*)* You're the top hat. You know you're the top hat.

TWEE. Maybe I want to change things up?

ROD. I already called it. JJ?

> (JJ *stares blankly at the pieces, as he has been this whole time.* **TWEE** *grabs the top hat.)*

JJ, come on. Which piece?

TWEE. *(To* **MOMO**.*)* Why the iron? No one wants the iron.

MOMO. Maybe you should switch to the dog, by which I mean bitch.

VERA. *(Scolding but also chuckling.)* Momo…

MOMO. *(Not really apologizing.)* Sorry.

> *(The board is almost set up…)*

ROD. JJ?

JJ. What? I don't care.

ROD. Battleship.

JJ. Fine.

VERA. I'll take the bitch. She's cute.

> (**VERA** *places $500 in the center of the board.)*

TWEE. No no no no no.

VERA. Why?

TWEE. Official rules only. If you land on property and don't buy it, it goes to auction. No rent if you don't ask for it. Your only option if you run out of cash is mortgaging or selling assets. Property surrendered to the bank by a bankrupt player immediately goes to auction. And no free money on Free Parking.

VERA. We always play this way.

TWEE. You do, the game never ends, and then you complain about it going too long. Official game rules. Vote: official rules only?

> (**TWEE**, **ROD**, *and* **MOMO** *raise their hands.)*

VERA. House rules.

(**VERA** *raises her hand.*)

VERA. *(Cont.)* JJ didn't vote.

TWEE. You lost anyway.

VERA. Hay naku. JJ – come on. Just Free Parking, nothing else special.

JJ. What?

VERA. Free Parking!

JJ. Oh. Just a free space. No benefits or penalties. Nothing. For anyone.

(*Pause.*)

ROD. What's wrong with you? Seriously?

JJ. Nothing. Ness.

ROD. What?

JJ. Nothing. What's wrong with you?

(**ROD** *rolls a die.*)

ROD. Four. Someone stole my brother and replaced him with some guy who lives on my couch.

(**MOMO** *rolls.*)

MOMO. Three.

JJ. You want me to leave?

ROD. No, obviously. But aren't you bigger than two books? All those comic conventions, the commissions for paintings and drawings, the movie stuff.

(**TWEE** *rolls.*)

TWEE. Shit. Three.

VERA. Language.

ROD. Why are you playing Contest of Champions all day instead of getting back on your feet?

JJ. You asked me to stay when I left LA and Henry \ started getting all –

ROD. That wasn't permission to turn my living room into a kingdom of epic loserdom.

(**VERA** *rolls.*)

VERA. Five.

JJ. You need privacy for a little rebound wham-bam-Grindr-man?

ROD. I have never used Grindr.

VERA. *(Holding the die out to JJ.)* What is this Grindr?

JJ. Of course you haven't!

VERA. Is it for sandwiches?

MOMO. Yes.

JJ. Mr. Rod-not-Toto is too good for the name his mother gave him and for social media.

ROD. Mom gave me BOTH names, I just prefer one over the other now!

VERA. Enough fighting.

JJ. I'll pack up tonight.

VERA. *(Insisting with the die.)* JJ!

ROD. I don't want you to leave. Just stop making me do this on my own. Dad, the \ hospital, and –

JJ. I'm not making you do anything. Just don't do it. Just stop.

ROD. I can't do that.

JJ. Yes, you can. Leave Dad alone, leave me alone, just stop. You even sound like him now!

VERA. Both of you: stop fighting or go back to your apartment! I'm not having this in my house.

> *(**ROD** and JJ back off. JJ rolls the die.)*

JJ. Five. We have to re-roll.

VERA. No. You go first. How's your dad?

> *(JJ starts his turn.)*

JJ. Good, I mean, no. He's stable now. Henry told Rod he's stable.

ROD. He is.

JJ. And he's out of the ICU, but he's still in the hospital indefinitely. So even though he's stable, it's a stretch to say he's good.

(JJ *moves his piece.*)

MOMO. Vermont Avenue. You want to buy it?

JJ. But when was he ever good, right? He's bad, you know, he's kind of bad. A bad person. And now, apparently, Toto wants to take his place. To be in charge. Except the person he thinks he's replacing was pretty bad at being in charge. Our dad is a bad dad for sure, a bad man in a lot of ways, and a bad person in even more, and this is my last chance to say it, isn't it? Because once he's gone, we'll have to remember him fondly. We'll have to say good shit about him, even though there's so little good shit to say, and a lot more shitty shit to say about the abusive, possibly mentally ill piece of crazy who is my father.

(**VERA** *smacks* **JJ.**)

VERA. The first six months my husband and I were here, your father and mother let us sleep in the little bedroom they used as an office until we got an apartment. He had a difficult life back home and it made him a difficult man – I'm not stupid. But he still put food on your plate, a roof over your head, and money in your pocket. And he is proud of you! You don't have to like him, but you do have to be grateful. There. There's some "good shit" for you to say.

(*Ten seconds.*)

JJ. I need some air.

(JJ *exits the apartment.*)

MOMO. He could have at least put it up for auction first.

VERA. Hay, just auction it.

TWEE. Those aren't the rules. Anyway, he'd be allowed to bid, if it were auctioned.

MOMO. Do you think he'll come back?

ROD. Take him out of the game.

TWEE. Go get him.

ROD. No. I'm not – I'm not running after him anymore.

TWEE. Text him and see if he still wants to play.

VERA. No. My house, my rules. Take him out.

TWEE. Seriously?

VERA. This – tonight is our chance to be normal. To play games like always. For me to get bored halfway through, leave, and start making snacks. For you and your brother to stay too late. So everyone, let's just play. I have work tomorrow.

TWEE. At least text him.

VERA. No. He needs time, not games. My house. My rules. He's out.

> (**VERA** *removes* **JJ***'s piece from the board and puts a $500 bill in its center.* **TWEE** *gets up.*)

TWEE. Fuck this.

VERA. Language. Where are you going?

TWEE. Out.

> (**TWEE** *exits.* **MOMO**, **ROD**, *and* **VERA** *look at each other.*)

MOMO. Maybe we could…you could teach us mahjong? Mom?

End of Scene

Scene Five

(JJ *on the roof of the building. His phone is in hand, but he stares out over the city instead.*)

(**TWEE** *enters.* JJ *quickly looks down at his phone.*)

TWEE. Fuck 'em all, right?

(JJ *stays focussed on his phone, barely acknowledging her.*)

Your phone is more fascinating than me? Wait, I rank lower than sudoku.

JJ. I need something that makes sense. Whereas you... people in general...

TWEE. Are not sudoku. I still don't understand the appeal.

JJ. In sudoku every question can be answered in a nine-by-nine grid, unlike the question, "Why would someone blow an entire grant on one trip to India?" which cannot.

TWEE. Sure it can. Write these letters in the top line: F-U-C-K – E-M – A-L-L.

JJ. Momo?

TWEE. All of them. They think they're such hot shit: living the American Dream – our parents' version of it, anyway. Doctors and nurses every one.
Fuck that and fuck them.
We all think we're so great because we grew up in this city, but honestly – until you've walked one block in Mumbai – you've got no clue how busy, disgusting, and exciting a city can be. It was another world.

JJ. Like Manila?

TWEE. No, totally different. India was gorgeous – I've got exhibitions upon exhibitions worth of pictures. Maybe some images to sell to stock agencies. I lived a life I knew nothing about. It was new.

JJ. New to you. Old to someone else.

(*A beat.*)

TWEE. My parents were miserable the entire time they lived in your parents' spare room. They used to make jokes about it. And your dad drives my mom insane; that's why she hasn't visited him at the hospital. Just like you haven't. Right? You haven't visited your dad. *(Pause.)* Just a hunch.

JJ. I can't take all the bitter, negative bile that spews out of him.

TWEE. Daddy's favorite son has abandoned him. I wish I had a set like yours. Some spectacular, testacular testicles. Instead I head home penniless and lick my overbearing cow of a mom's ass so I can sleep in my old room.

JJ. I'm on Toto's couch.

TWEE. And why does Mr. Goody Two Shoes let you get away with not visiting pappy-san?

JJ. Is there anyone you don't absolutely detest?

TWEE. You're not half bad. You and I actually made our own way. Plus, this whole not visiting your dad thing is pretty awesome.

JJ. That is not awesome.

TWEE. Your dad is a tool, JJ. Fuck him.

JJ. He's always been good to me, though.

TWEE. Being good to you at the expense of others is still being a complete cock. Look at my mom. I am an amazing woman, JJ. But she throws all of her disapproval and disappointment at me while doting on mousey, friendless, little ol' Momo as though she were god's gift, and I were devil's spawn. And Mo loves her for it.

Your dad adores you, and he's a dick to Toto. But you know he's a nasty, bitter old man, regardless of how differently he treats you – BECAUSE of how differently he treats you. If Mo were a real sister to me just once, looked out for me…sometimes I need a sister.

JJ. You don't look like you need anyone.

TWEE. You're not looking hard enough.

JJ. No one – most people usually don't.

TWEE. Fuck them, too.

JJ. Fuck 'em all.

TWEE. I see you, JJ.

JJ. These days I have trouble seeing myself. What do you see?

TWEE. A dude who lost his job and almost lost his dad in the same week, who can't handle when circumstances that should bring him closer to his family make him hide on the roof instead.

JJ. You're up on the roof, too.

TWEE. I am, because you're hiding something else. I'm trying to figure out what it is.

JJ. Look harder.

> (**TWEE** *looks at* **JJ**. *He turns and looks back at her.*)

TWEE. Not your brother… Not your dad… Your job –?

> (**JJ** *kisses* **TWEE**. *He jumps back.*)

JJ. Sorry.

> (**TWEE** *kisses* **JJ**. *It's a good kiss.*)

TWEE. Huh. That wasn't half bad. Not true love, but not bad.

Let's do this. But not, for the love of god, on your brother's couch.

JJ. Excuse me?

TWEE. Trust me, I don't usually open with, "Let's do this. Not on your brother's couch." But sometimes you have to write the answers outside of the nine-by-nine grid. Plus, we've known each other forever, and for at least seven years of that forever, you've wanted to know me, biblically.

JJ. You're staying at your parents'.

TWEE. Shit. Stairwell?

JJ. We'll get caught.

TWEE. So?

JJ. So…
BOTH. Fuck 'em all.

End of Scene

Scene Six

(**MOMO** *and* **HENRY** *sitting in a hospital break room.* **MOMO** *is in front of her laptop with a VoIP headset on.* **HENRY** *watches her.*)

(*They both eat lunches.*)

MOMO. (*To the computer.*) Lumalangoy ang mga batang babae. [Translation: The girls swim.]

HENRY. (*Quietly to himself.*) Lu…malang…oy. Lumalangoy.

MOMO. (*To the computer.*) Tumatakbo ang lalaki. [The boy runs.]

HENRY. (*Quietly.*) Lalaki.

MOMO. (*To the computer.*) Naglalakad ang babae at ang mga batang lalaki. [The woman and the boys walk.]

HENRY. (*Glancing at her screen.*) Naglalakad ang babae at ang mga –

(**MOMO** *takes off the headset.*)

MOMO. What?

HENRY. Batang…what?

MOMO. Were you talking?

HENRY. Yeah, no. Not really.

(**MOMO** *puts the headset back on.*)

(*Quietly.*) Naglalakad ang babae at ang mga batang lalaki.

(**MOMO** *takes off the headset and looks at him.*)

Does that program really work?

MOMO. It's structured like a fun memory game, so I learn things before I even realize it. Right now I'm matching sentences to pictures. But I don't know yet. Ask me in a year.

HENRY. I've always wondered what it would be like to learn.

MOMO. Toto is fluent in Tagalog. You were together for four years.

HENRY. I guess I never thought he'd want to teach me, but you're so into it. Learning a language at an age when our brains are no longer in the best place to... Doing new things... It's really cool.

MOMO. Ask Toto to teach you.

HENRY. He doesn't want to do anything. With me.

MOMO. Why?

(**HENRY** *takes a bite of his lunch. Chews...then:*)

HENRY. Never mind.

(**MOMO** *puts the headset back on.*)

MOMO. *(To the computer.)* Tumatakbo ang kabayo. [The horse runs.]

HENRY. *(Quietly.)* Kabayo. Ang kabayo.

MOMO. Shut up.

HENRY. Shut –

(**MOMO** *rips off the headset.*)

MOMO. HENRY, STOP IT.

HENRY. I didn't think you could hear me.

MOMO. Yes, you did. Next time you want my attention just try, "Hey, Mo. What's up?"

HENRY. Well...sooooo, what's up?

MOMO. Maybe if you and Toto get back together, this new creeper persona of yours will recede back into the swamp from which it came. Check into that, maybe.

HENRY. I mean, Toto and I... I'm not really sure about stuff. And it's not fair for me to – he needs...

MOMO. Sure about what?

HENRY. He needs people who are sure.

(**ROD** *enters.*)

ROD. *(To the room.)* Hey.

MOMO. Hey.

(*To* **HENRY.**)

About what?

HENRY. Never mind.

ROD. *(To* **HENRY**, *pointedly.)* Hey.

HENRY. Hey.

> *(***HENRY** *smiles as he picks up his lunch and exits.)*

ROD. Sorry I said, "Hey," like a work colleague instead of running out of the room like an ex-boyfriend with the maturity of a high school freshman. He can show up to a private gathering, but he can't share a semi-public space?

MOMO. He can't handle how much he wants you.

ROD. Did you not just witness that?

MOMO. What happened between you and Henry?

ROD. Stop talking about it. How's my dad?

MOMO. I haven't been by. He doesn't need neurology. Everything wrong with his brain was already wrong when he got here.

ROD. Don't. He's my dad.

MOMO. Oh, right, your dad. The man who threw me out of your house once when he thought I would trick you into impregnating me and prevent you from going to medical school? That dad?

ROD. I know.

MOMO. You never would have gotten into med school if I hadn't been tutoring you in Chem.

ROD. I know, I know.

MOMO. *(Impersonating* **ERNIE.**) "Leave and take that dirty pussy trap with you!"

ROD. Oh, god. I'm so sorry. Forever and always. But he's sick now. We should think nice things about him, or whatever, until his condition improves.

MOMO. He doesn't deserve you.

ROD. What did I just say?

MOMO. That wasn't a mean thing about him. That was a nice thing about you.

ROD. Mmmmm…somehow you're wrong. I haven't figured out how, but you are.

MOMO. It's my dirty pussy trap tricking you.

ROD. Okay, see, making fun of him – even indirectly – is definitely bad. You're sending bad energy his way.

MOMO. When did we become hippies, Toto?

ROD. Rod.

MOMO. ROD. I've known you so long as… I'm trying.

ROD. We've known each other for a long time. Yes. So maybe you can tell me why the hell I'm thinking about energy? Why I'm taking such good care of him instead of letting his actual doctors do their jobs? Why I'm neither falling apart completely nor telling my dad to fuck off like any sane person would? Like he deserves.

MOMO. You're not doing it because he does or doesn't deserve it. You're doing it, because you're a good son regardless.

ROD. Paano mo sabihin, "thank you"?

MOMO. Salamat…po?

ROD. Oo. "Po." Salamat po. Well done.

MOMO. Yeah. This program is actually fun, so I don't even \ know I'm –

ROD. *(Suddenly.)* The day before my dad's heart attack, Henry proposed to me. And then the next week, a week later, we broke up. He said he couldn't marry me.

MOMO. What?

ROD. Henry dumped me.

MOMO. No, no, no. The first part. He proposed? Marriage. Why didn't you tell me?

ROD. It didn't seem right to say anything while my dad was dying. And then after he got better, Henry broke it off. I was, I don't know, embarrassed? Ashamed? Ashamed. I thought I fucked something up. That I did something.

MOMO. Which is why you tell me, so I can tell you that you didn't do anything.

(A beat.)

ROD. I'm going to check on Dad, and then... I have rounds.

> **(ROD** *exits.)*
>
> **(MOMO** *sits eating for a moment, taking it in.)*
>
> *(And then...quietly...* **HENRY** *comes back in. He sits in his former seat and resumes eating his lunch.* **MOMO** *stares at him. He smiles self-consciously at her. She keeps staring.)*

HENRY. Your question. About Rod and me...? If Rod got sick, I'm not sure I could... And life is...there are so many things I still want – I mean, I've always been a little bisexual, even.

> *(A beat.)*
>
> **(MOMO** *shuts her laptop.)*

MOMO. What?

HENRY. What?

MOMO. Are you hitting on me?

HENRY. No. I was just –

MOMO. Henry. I don't care. Don't tell me any of this. Don't "accidentally" show up at my house. Don't make me your substitute or intermediary. Stop this cowardly creeper stuff, man up, and go after what you really want, boldly, while there's still a sliver of a chance you might get it.

> **(MOMO** *exits.)*
>
> **(HENRY** *sighs. He takes a bite of his lunch, considering boldness.)*

End of Scene

Scene Seven

*(*VERA *teaching* MOMO *and* TWEE *how to play mahjong.)*

VERA. Mahjong is basically a card game with tiles instead of cards. Each game has three rounds. First, we set up, which is like dealing the cards, but even "the deal" has rules. We roll dice to see who goes first, and then the first player rolls again. We count off that number counter-clockwise from the first player to determine who picks the flower wall. Then, we draw tiles from the remaining walls – eight tiles the first time around, nine the second.

MOMO. Eight plus nine?

VERA. Yes. Then once we have \ the tiles –

MOMO. Seventeen tiles.

VERA. Right.

MOMO. I thought mahjong was thirteen tiles. Or fourteen?

VERA. This version is seventeen.

TWEE. What version? Your version?

VERA. Not "my" version. Filipino mahjong.

TWEE. Filipino as opposed to…?

VERA. Chinese.

TWEE. No, no, no, no, no, lady. Mahjong is from China. We're learning the Chinese rules. None of your tricks.

VERA. "Lady."

MOMO. Mom, can we learn the basics first?

VERA. These are the basics of Filipino mahjong.

TWEE. Good god, woman.

VERA. "Lady," "woman!" Tweety Bird, repeat after me: "Thank you."

TWEE. Thank you.

VERA. "For teaching me."

TWEE. For teaching me.

VERA. "Dearest mother of mine."

TWEE. Dearest, sweetest, bestest mother of my heart.

VERA. You need to learn to follow directions, but that's okay for now.

MOMO. I want to learn the right way before I learn any variations.

TWEE. What she said.

VERA. This is the right way. For Filipinos. When you asked me to teach you to cook arroz caldo, you didn't ask for the right way. You asked for my way.

MOMO. Because there is no right way to cook it.

VERA. No – because you wanted to learn what I cook. So now I'm going to teach you how I play. Not how Chinese people or American people play.

TWEE. We should learn American rules. We're in America.

VERA. Hay naku. Those rules need four players anyway. With Filipino rules, you can play only three.

MOMO. Dad's just watching TV.

VERA. No. He'll only play if there's money.

TWEE. Ooooo… I like the sound of that.

VERA. No gambling today.

MOMO. You don't have any money, anyway.

TWEE. We could ask Sheila to come over.

MOMO. What?

TWEE. She could be our fourth.

MOMO. Or Rod.

VERA. Why Rod, ha? Again Rod. All the time Rod. Again.

MOMO. He just went through a bad breakup.

TWEE. And now you think it's a good time to finally snatch him up?

MOMO. No.

VERA. He's a good man, and he's a doctor.

MOMO. I'm a doctor. And he's cardiology, whereas I'm neurology, so I'm a sexier doctor than he is.

VERA. Hay, Momo.

MOMO. And you know our friendship isn't like that.

VERA. Right. Because he's...

> (**VERA** *holds up her arm and makes her wrist limp.* **TWEE** *laughs.*)

MOMO. Mom, stop it.

VERA. You know, in the Philippines we didn't have gay.

MOMO. STOP. Yes, you did.

VERA. I didn't know any gay people until we moved here. And then I started work at the hospital and all of the non-Filipino male nurses were gay! So many all of a sudden. And you know what? They are very good nurses. I don't know about cardiologists...

TWEE. Tito Telly is gay, and he's from the Philippines.

VERA. But he wasn't gay there. Only here.

MOMO. No! You just didn't know.

VERA. No. He was straight in the Philippines, but he moved here for a nursing job and he is a very good nurse, so he became a gay to fit in with all of the other very good nurses.

MOMO. MOM, that is completely ridiculous. Do you even know how ignorant...

> (**MOMO** *realizes that* **VERA** *is chuckling to herself.*)

You are a terrible mother.

VERA. I have been living in this city for more than thirty years! Why do you act like I climbed out of a rice paddy yesterday? You and your sister! How did I raise two girls to be just like their father? Humorless.

TWEE. I'm not humorless. I'm here for fun, so let's call Sheila and get on with it.

MOMO. Fine, fine, fine. Filipino rules.

VERA. Call her, if you want.

MOMO. She's working today.

TWEE. You're such a push over.

> (**MOMO** *rolls her eyes.*)

MOMO. Ugh. Shut up.

TWEE. You look like a frog when you do that.

MOMO. Shut up. I do not.

TWEE. You look like a frog.

VERA. Twee.

TWEE. Do it again. You do! Do it.

> (**MOMO** *rolls her eyes out of annoyance, not because she's following* **TWEE***'s instructions. When she realizes she's done it, she freezes, trying to picture her own face.*)

See, see, see! Dearest mother, look.

VERA. Hmmm.

TWEE. Ribbit.

> (**VERA** *starts to laugh.*)

MOMO. Mom!

VERA. It's funny! You look a little bit like a frog.

TWEE. An anime frog.

MOMO. Can we just learn the game? Three people. Filipino rules.

TWEE. Four people. The real rules. Call Sheila.

VERA. That's enough, Twee.

TWEE. I don't get why Sheila can't just come over. I mean, Mo, you're here at Mom's all the time now. Do you just leave Sheila alone all day?

MOMO. She's at work.

TWEE. If I were your roommate, I'd – she's your "roommate," right? Sheila's your "roommate"?

MOMO. I mean, we live –

TWEE. Right.

VERA. Twee.

TWEE. I would think something was up. Or is it some arrangement where you barely see each other. Is Sheila good with that? Barely talk to each other. Barely touch \ each –

MOMO. Oh, my god.

VERA. Leave your sister alone now.

TWEE. I'm trying to learn about her life. About what she does when she's not hiding out underneath mommy dearest's skirts trying to be your mini-me.

VERA. Maybe she's not ready to talk to you about her life.

TWEE. Stop coddling her.

MOMO. I'm not the one living in my old bedroom.

TWEE. Oh, here we go!

MOMO. Who's the one with a real job? And her own apartment? If anyone's hiding under Mom's skirts, it's you.

TWEE. Fine! Then I'll leave!

VERA. What?

MOMO. GOOD!

TWEE. I'll pack right now.

VERA. Momo, stop this –

TWEE. No, it's fine! You think I didn't know there would be consequences to pissing away my grant? You think I don't want to be a better photographer than I am, that I'm happy making most of my money selling stock photos and taking people's head shots? I don't need to stay here and listen to the queen of losers tell me to bow!

VERA. Both of you stop yelling and listen to me.

TWEE. Don't deny it or anything, woman. I hear you both tittering in the corner, talking about what to do with me. You're on her side. You're always on her side!

VERA. You're staying here, aren't you?

TWEE. And the pair of you won't let me forget it!

VERA. You're staying here, because I love you. And I won't let you forget it, because I love you! The only one who doesn't seem to love you is you.

MOMO. I don't.

VERA. Monica.

MOMO. I really think at this point I have stopped loving you.

TWEE. I'm glad you finally admitted it.

VERA. Monica, apologize to your sister.

MOMO. I'm not sorry. You're shallow, heartless, and arrogant.

TWEE. You're boring, insecure, and cowardly.

MOMO. Mom does everything for you, and you're totally ungrateful.

TWEE. If she didn't hold you up, you'd ooze away like a river of diarrhea.

VERA. Stop it!

MOMO. You don't know CRAP about me, you stupid, filthy bitch!

> (**VERA** smacks **MOMO**. *Not hard – just enough to get both their attentions.*)

VERA. Apologize to your sister.

MOMO. …What?

VERA. You don't love her? You love her! Apologize.

MOMO. I…sorry.

> *(Pause.)*

VERA. Twee?

> *(Pause.)*

TWEE. Ribbit.

VERA. You are a bitch.

TWEE. Mom!

VERA. You both think I'm going to be here forever to stand between you. But I could die soon, like Ernie is dying! And what do I have to show for it?

The two of you.

Do you think it was easy to come here and leave everything I know? To have you here instead of back home surrounded by my sisters? I wish they could have been here to help me and show me what to do, but instead I broke all the rules and made up some new ones so you could have a good education, a good home, a good life. And now you are like this.

(To TWEE.*)*

You think she's insecure? So are you!

(To MOMO.*)*

You think she's heartless? So are you!

I came here so you could be better than me. Happier than me. So you could take the rules I made up and come up with your own. Instead all you do is show me how you can't stand each other. How leaving my family was a mistake, because now you don't know how to be one. How I failed as a mother.

I failed.

(A beat.)

MOMO. Mom, you haven't –

VERA. Leave me alone now, Momo.

TWEE. Stop being so dramatic, \ Mom.

VERA. JOSEPHINE.

Both of you. Come back when we can play this game together. Right now, get out of my sight.

*(*TWEE *pushes over her tiles and storms off.* MOMO *starts to pick them up, but* VERA *smacks her hands away.)*

*(*MOMO *slinks off as tears streak down her face.)*

(When they're gone, VERA *takes a deep breath and rubs her temples. She begins cleaning up the game, but she feels disoriented. One of her hands flops clumsily.)*

(There's a sharp flash of light, as VERA *gasps and looks up, pained.)*

End of Scene

Scene Eight

(**ROD** and **HENRY** at a pricey, chic Asian-fusion restaurant. Something like Buddakan. In fact, let's call it Boddhisattva.)

(**HENRY** is smiling. **ROD** is hostile.)

ROD. So.

HENRY. Hi.

ROD. Great.

HENRY. Hey.

ROD. So. Hi.

HENRY. How…

ROD. Here we are.

HENRY. How are you?

ROD. The real answer to that question in this context – sitting HERE with YOU – is so complex that I'm too exhausted to even think about blurting out the long, murderous rant.

HENRY. You love this place.

ROD. Sitting here with you, I'm starting to hate it.

HENRY. But those scallops with the ginger-miso stuff \ that –

ROD. Henry…

HENRY. You love that ginger –

ROD. Henry.

HENRY. Or that sea bass with the chilis, and –

ROD. HENRY, WHAT ARE WE DOING HERE?

HENRY. Talking…quietly. Not yelling.

ROD. This is like a date.

HENRY. You love this place, and I thought that \ we could –

ROD. You would ruin it for me? You would take your ex-almost-fiancé to his favorite restaurant, and piss on his heart while he enjoyed haute cuisine, pan-Asian fucking seafood?

HENRY. Toto, please calm down.

ROD. ROD. I'm Rod.

HENRY. I'm tired of you being mad at me.

ROD. THEN STOP DOING THINGS THAT PISS ME OFF!

HENRY. Indoor voice!

ROD. You said we need to talk. You're right, we do. So invite me over to your pathetic new bachelor pad or grab coffee with me. Don't take me to a fancy dinner, wearing that shirt I bought you that still looks really good on you and smile like this is a date. Not a post-breakup, post-dissolved engagement talk – a date. A good date.

HENRY. I just want you to be happy. To make you happy.

ROD. You making me happy makes me really fucking sad now. You can't come back from what you've done.

HENRY. Oh. Ever?

ROD. No. So talk, or else let's go. We're both on call, anyway.

HENRY. But I... I didn't really have anything to talk about. I just wanted to do something nice for you.

ROD. Okay. Then stop stalking Mo. It's pissing me off, and it's creeping her out. That would be nice. And withdraw your request to take care of my dad.

HENRY. Don't you want someone who cares about your dad to take care of him?

ROD. Not if that someone claimed to care about me and then left when things got scary. And since when do you care about my dad?

HENRY. I care because you do. I love you, Rod.

(*Pause.*)

ROD. Do not speak those words in that sequence ever again.

HENRY. It's true.

ROD. It's irrelevant if your feelings have no effect on your cowardly behavior.

HENRY. I know. I agree.

ROD. OH, PLEASE. DON'T EVEN START WITH – wait? You agree?

HENRY. Yes. I agree.

ROD. Good. Then promise to leave Momo, my dad, and me alone, and let's go home. I mean, let's leave.

HENRY. Your dad is sick, and you deserve better. Someone who could be better.

ROD. Bullshit. I don't need a hypothetical someone to be better. I need you, like I've always needed you, but you left!

HENRY. Toto, Ernie's heart stopped, his brain, all of his organs failed. I was at the hospital every day, imagining you losing him. Imagining losing you. Wondering whether I was good enough to make all those decisions about his life or yours.

And it wasn't enough to like the same movies, to tell you jokes that made you laugh, and to wake up next to you on a Wednesday morning, every morning for the rest of my life. It wasn't enough to be me. Suddenly, you needed a real boyfriend – fiancé.

I haven't slept with a woman in ten years, and sometimes I still want to. I dream of living in Australia. I come home from work knowing if I could go back in time, I never would have become a doctor. I have no idea what I want, or who I am.

So what if today I'm a good man, but tomorrow I fail, and next year I'm just a fucking horrible piece of shit?

Your father was dying. That's not what you needed. You needed all of that out of your way. So I broke it off. I broke it off because I didn't want to hurt you or fail you or lose you forever.

ROD. BUT YOU HAVE HURT ME AND FAILED ME, HENRY. You left when my father was dying. YOU DESERVE TO LOSE ME FOREVER!!

> (**HENRY** and **ROD** *stop. They look around the restaurant at the other diners.*)

(To the other diners.) Sorry, everyone.

HENRY. *(Also to the other diners.)* Nothing to worry about. Don't...we're doctors.

> *(They turn quietly back to each other.)*
>
> *(Five seconds.)*

Forever is pretty harsh. Pretty final.

ROD. Yes, it is. Final. Did you think we'd just be friends now?

HENRY. Well, you know, maybe.

ROD. All I want is for you to like a movie with me, tell me your stupid jokes, and wake up with me on a Wednesday. Don't sit there blaming your failure on my sudden, all too real need, when the only reason you failed is because you failed.

HENRY. Rod, I just – I panicked! I thought I was doing you a favor. I didn't realize it would pass, and that I could be there for you. I can be there for you. Now.

ROD. What about when I get old and sick? What will you do, Henry, when I'm the one lying in a hospital bed?

> *(Silence.)*

Withdraw your request for my father's case. Handle it tomorrow. First thing.

HENRY. Okay.

ROD. And leave Momo alone.

HENRY. Okay.

I'm sorry.

Forgive me.

ROD. Some other time, maybe I could have. But he's dying. He is a bitter man who never got what he wanted from life and blamed everyone else for it. Usually me. And if I can't make room to forgive my dying father, why the fuck should I forgive you?

> *(Both of their cell phones ring, simultaneously. They look to each other for a second, and then grab them.)*

HENRY. *(Looking at the caller ID.)* The hospital. Yours?

ROD. *(Looking at his.)* No. Momo…

    (They pick up.)

BOTH. Hello…?

End of Scene

Scene Nine

(JJ and **TWEE** *on* **ROD**'s *couch. They're in underwear, covered by a throw.)*

JJ. I spy with my little eye something green.

TWEE. The chair. NO – the cover on the armrest of the chair.

JJ. Very good.

TWEE. I'm in your brain now, Johan. No one is safe!

I spy with my BIG, BEAUTIFUL eye something aquamarine.

JJ. Aquamarine?

TWEE. You're the artist. You don't know what aquamarine is?

JJ. It's turquoise. You're more of an artist than I am.

TWEE. Sort of turquoise, but bluer and greener. Richer. Aquamarine.

JJ. Oh, Jesus. The, uh…that thing. The bud vase.

TWEE. Your turn.

JJ. I spy with my little eye something brown.

TWEE. Your brother's pretty butch in the decor department. At least give me a Crayola color or something.

JJ. Brown is a Crayola color.

TWEE. I hate you.

JJ. It is!

TWEE. My face.

JJ. Yup.

TWEE. Shut up!

JJ. No, really.

TWEE. My face is not a "thing." I'm a person.

JJ. But if I say, "I spy with my little eye some person who's brown," that kind of gives it away.

TWEE. And I'm not brown. I'm golden.

JJ. What are you, Latino?

*(**TWEE** becomes more and more hostile.)*

TWEE. What the fuck does that mean?

JJ. You know, with their million adjectives for distinguishing skin color.

TWEE. It's not a race thing.

JJ. Okay.

TWEE. I'm just not brown.

JJ. OKAY.

TWEE. What are you implying?

JJ. Nothing. This is all you, okay? Whatever is going through your brain right now is all coming from you.

TWEE. You implied with the Latino thing. That I'm racist.

JJ. WHOA – excuse me?

TWEE. They have all those different classifications for all the different skin tones to differentiate their skin from black skin, because they're racist. That's what you said.

JJ. I certainly did not.

TWEE. You implied.

JJ. No, I didn't! And I don't even think that's true. There are a lot of different skin tones, so it makes sense to be specific.

TWEE. Don't back pedal.

JJ. I never pedalled! This is not a bike!

*(**TWEE** pauses.)*

TWEE. Not a…not a bike.

JJ. No.

*(**TWEE** is quiet.)*

So…what's eating you?

TWEE. I don't know. I guess it means I have race issues, along with every other fucking thing that's supposed to be wrong with me, while sainted, flawless Momo is all about her roots all of a sudden. So she beat me again!

JJ. I think it means you have some insecurities.

TWEE. That's generous.

JJ. You could afford to be more generous. To yourself. And Mo.

TWEE. This über-Filipino thing is freaking me out. I mean, fine: the world is divided into things Twee does and things Momo does. As it always has been and ever shall be, Amen. She becomes a doctor and never leaves some twenty blocks and is close to Mom, and I fly to India and have gallery shows and cringe when our parents open their mouths. That is the natural order.

But why does she get to be the one who learns Tagalog and how to cook sinigang? I mean the other day she's spraying Flip-juice out of every pore, so I go, "What the fuck?" And she says – you know what Mo says to me? "Our parents won't be around forever." What can you say to that? She stakes her claim, then erects an impassable fence on its border, and posts a big fucking sign: "Our parents will die, and I'm the one who gets to remember them."

And now she gets to think she's better than me again, when really she's just as lost as I am. Cooking fish soup and saying "Mabuhay!" won't keep anyone from dying.

JJ. Twee, learn Tagalog if you want to learn. Whoever Mo is or you are, there's no natural order to maintain.

TWEE. That's easy for you to say. You and Toto actually take care of each other.

JJ. No. It's not. Knowing that nothing matters is not "easy."

TWEE. What the hell is that supposed to mean?

JJ. I was the artist on *Victory Society,* you know? In comics, it's a big deal. My re-designs of Action, Calliope, Frost, Flame, and Odeon have established their look for the decade to come, at least. They even hired me to work with the production designer for the movie adaptation. That's how I bought my condo in LA. I'm living the dream, right? Not just surviving on drawing – thriving. So one day I'm totally in the zone, drawing a page for *Victory Society,* and it hits me: nothing has changed.

TWEE. Sounds like a lot changed.

JJ. I worked two years as JUST an artist in my tricked out office, living my dream, but women still confuse me. Politics still infuriate me. My mother is still a stress case. My father is still a sociopath. And once a year a random moment in a movie – typically involving a talking animal – will spontaneously make me cry.

I have it all and nothing changed.

I could lose it all and nothing will change.

I could die, and the universe would keep spinning its out of control spin.

I snapped out of it and realized that I pencilled every character completely naked. Breasts, dicks, vaginas, asses.

I even invented genitalia for the aliens the Victory Society was fighting in my moment of – what...?

Collapse. I collapsed. And I keep on collapsing – realizing that the things I believe define me are paper thin illusions. So thin looking at them is enough to make them dissolve.

I'm dissolving. And no one notices.

Then my dad got sick. He was dying without having figured out how to live. And I thought: that's me. So I left it all. My life. One suitcase and the shirt on my back. And here I am on Toto's couch.

TWEE. I spy with my little eye one pathetic loser piece of shit. Does Rod know this?

JJ. I told him I was fired.

Learn Tagalog, Twee. There's no natural order. It's all chaos. Learn if you want to learn.

TWEE. JJ, everyone collapses once in awhile. Then you fuck the wrong dude or drink an entire bottle of the hard stuff and get back up again.

JJ. Or fly to India?

TWEE. Whatever. But when you collapse AND THEN get a boulder thrown on you, you've got to push that fucking boulder off, then fuck the dude or drink the shit, then get up.

JJ. What in the name of Christ are you saying?

TWEE. Parental mortality would shake up anyone. The fact that you were already vulnerable when Ernie's ticker decided not to tock is amplifying completely normal feelings.

I mean, I could give a rat's ass about your dad. But this shit was still a sign for me: fuck 'em all. Do what I need to do with my grant, mooch off my mom.

Push off that boulder and visit your dad.

JJ. It's not like he'll have any answers.

TWEE. Then just to tell him to fuck off.

JJ. That's not the solution to every problem, and I thought you liked that I haven't visited my dad.

TWEE. I liked it when it was because you were a badass. When it's because you're an incapacitated pussy ass coward, it's less sexy.

JJ. Is this the part where I realize I'm fucking the wrong dude?

TWEE. There's another dude here? Why am I not getting tag-teamed?

JJ. I meant the brown dude who can't stop spewing vulgarities. That dude.

TWEE. That dude is totally the wrong dude.

JJ. The guy who walked out on his life – he's probably the wrong dude, too. For you.

TWEE. I know. I'm not stupid.

JJ. I know.

> (**TWEE** *and* **JJ** *start to make out.*)

TWEE. You know this couch? It's not a bad couch after all.

JJ. Yeah, well, just don't tell –

> (*The sound of a door opening.* **ROD** *enters with a furious urgency, and then stops and stares, stunned.*)

> (**TWEE** *gets up and starts dressing with a what-a-pain-in-the-ass deliberateness. She's not rushing; she knows they've been caught.*)

(Ten seconds.)

TWEE. Yes. We're fucking. Jesus.

ROD. Oh.

JJ. Rod.

ROD. JJ.

(Silence.)

TWEE. What have you got, Rod? Ready to lay into your brother for screwing the Anti-Christ? And on your five thousand dollar couch!

ROD. I…no.

(Silence.)

JJ. What?

ROD. Why didn't you answer your phone?

JJ. I was…busy. What's wrong?

(Silence.)

Is Dad –?

ROD. Dad is – Dad's fine.

*(**ROD** looks to **TWEE**.)*

TWEE. What?

ROD. Mo's been calling you. She's…at the hospital.

End of Scene

Scene Ten

(The hospital break room. **MOMO** *and* **TWEE** *sit at opposing ends of the space.* **JJ** *lingers in the back, more on* **TWEE***'s side.* **ROD** *is between the sisters, looking from one to the other.)*

ROD. Vera is stable enough for surgery, but she's not conscious or responsive. Your dad refuses to leave her, so Henry is keeping him company. They'll be prepping her for the operation soon, so it's a good time for your dad to take a break, if you think you can get him in here.

MOMO. It was an ICH?

ROD. Yes. So they'll attempt to evacuate the hematoma.

MOMO. Thanks, Toto. I mean –

ROD. It's fine.

TWEE. I don't understand.

ROD. There was a ballooned blood vessel in Vera's brain, and its subsequent hemorrhaging caused –

TWEE. No, I understand the science. Despite my MFA, I don't need cartoons and soothing narration to understand an aneurysm. What I don't understand is how my mother could suffer a stroke when her dear, sweet, number one daughter is a goddamn neurologist.

(Silence.)

Momo, that obvious barb has dug its thorns in, and is now hanging off your slack-jawed, stony fucking face.

(Ten seconds and then **MOMO** *starts crying.)*

What good is that doing? Stop fucking crying and go help our mother!

ROD. The doctors with her now are the best we've got.

TWEE. Better than Mo?

ROD. Comparable.

TWEE. Compare me to a unicorn. That doesn't make me a magical fertility beast with a phallus sticking out of my forehead.

ROD. No, you have two horns, cloven hooves, and a pointy tail.

TWEE. Oh, good! At least someone in this room can react appropriately.

ROD. Mo's mother is hospitalized, too. Maybe you could commiserate or at least put a lid on it until we have a clearer picture of how this will go.

TWEE. I'll put a lid on it when my wussy baby sister grows an ass spine and attends to her precious mother.

MOMO. Stop calling her that.

TWEE. SHE SPEAKS! Now up. Up, up, skedaddle!

MOMO. We already know how this will go. Our precious mother will die.

ROD. We don't know that.

MOMO. She had an aneurysm resulting in a hemorrhagic stroke, in a half hour window between when we left her and Dad found her. Who knows when in that window it actually happened. It's a miracle she survived long enough to get to the hospital! For her to make it through AND wake up AND even be a shadow version of the woman she was are four more miracles than we deserve to expect.

TWEE. Fuck what I deserve! Go in there and expect miracles, whether we get them or not. She is your mom – MY MOM.

MOMO. Just because you can't do anything, doesn't mean you can expect me to fix it all for you!

TWEE. Mo, we both already know I'm as useful as tits on a snake here. You have a sliver of a chance to make this good, so you have to be the one who's good at this, because you already are.

And if you don't go in there now and help, just help – even if you don't succeed – if you don't even try, you can bet that I will make your life a living fucking hell until the day one or both of us leaves this goddamn shit earth. You won't be able to get dressed, cook pancit, learn Tagalog, do your ratty hair, or even breathe without hearing the echoes of my harpy screeches in your head. You will never stop hearing me harangue you about getting a man, even when you finally grow some ovaries and tell me you've been bumping uglies with Sheila, because I'll tell you it's just a phase that'll be cured the minute you get your first taste of rock hard man cock. Little Miss Monica, I will fuck your life until it screams like the dry, frigid, drum tight twat that you –

> (**MOMO** *smacks* **TWEE** *across the face.*)

> (*A beat.*)

Ready?

MOMO. Come with me.

TWEE. But I'm useless.

MOMO. No, you're not. Please?

> (**TWEE** *nods. They exit together.*)

ROD. I will never…

JJ. What?

ROD. And now you are…

JJ. WHAT?

ROD. …Nothing.

> (*Pause.*)

Dad is on seven. Room 722.

JJ. That did occur to me.

> (*Pause.*)

ROD. You and Twee…?

JJ. Not long. A couple weeks.

ROD. Totally new?

JJ. Yeah. Weird at first, but…good. I think.

ROD. I see very little of Twee that I would characterize as good.

JJ. Mo's in there, isn't she? Not out here, hopeless. If you really listen to the things Twee says, she can be really – I don't know – motivating. And funny, actually.

ROD. How motivating? Does she know you haven't visited Dad?

JJ. She was just calling me an incapacitated pussy ass coward when you found us.

ROD. I…am not mad at that.

>   *(A beat.)*

JJ, there are no second chances after this.

JJ. He's an evil, evil man, Rod.

ROD. Who is our dad. Who loves you.

JJ. Because I don't stand up to him! It's not love or care; it's the path of least resistance.

ROD. Well, eventually you won't have the choice to stand up to him or not.

JJ. So? They left us stumbling around to figure life out on our own – Dad being Dad; Mom back home with Lola forgetting she ever met him. I don't owe him a visit. I don't owe him anything.

ROD. I don't care about him or what he's "owed."

Fine, he didn't show us how to live, but that doesn't mean we can't live, and we definitely can't avoid life. Who do you think will be in charge when he's actually gone? Or who'll change their entire life to take care of him if he gets out of here? Life will happen whether we want it to or not, and we need to learn the rules of whatever new game it throws our way. I do. But even though I know that, I still end up acting like a child. Keeping secrets. Blaming the people closest to me for my problems. Pushing them away. I end up exactly like him.

And I'm actually visiting him every day, wrestling with how not to be him. You need to make peace with who he is before the chance passes you by.

JJ. You're not him.

ROD. You said it. I sound like him.

JJ. I mean, you're being an asshole, but you're not pushing me away. Who do you think you're pushing –?

> (**HENRY** *enters.* **ROD** *immediately bristles with hostility.*)

HENRY. Hey.

ROD. HENRY, could you leave me alone for just five fucking minutes, you useless piece of shit?

> (*A beat.*)

HENRY. Okay. I… Mo's with Vera now, and Twee's with their dad in the waiting room. I thought you'd want to know. And that I would maybe check on you.

ROD. Right.

HENRY. Let me know if you need anything.

> (**HENRY** *goes. Ten seconds.*)

JJ. Room 722.

ROD. Yeah.

> (**JJ** *starts to go and then turns back to* **ROD.**)

JJ. I wasn't fired. From *Victory Society* or *Odeon.* I walked out.

ROD. They'll take you back, won't they?

JJ. Probably. I'm hot shit. Maybe not those books, but on a lesser title to boost sales. And they'll probably need me in post for the movie.

ROD. Good.

JJ. Should I go back?

ROD. Yes.

JJ. I feel like you knew.

ROD. I wondered. I mean, you're hot shit.

JJ. Then why did you let me do that to your living room?

ROD. You needed help. You're my brother.

> (**JJ** *hugs* **ROD.**)

JJ. Love you.

ROD. I love you, too.

End of Scene

Scene Eleven

(JJ and ERNIE *in Room 722.* ERNIE *is definitely a bit drugged now. He remains onstage in his hospital bed until the end of the play.)*

ERNIE. I always miss you. I ask the nurses, "Where's my son?" And they always tell me you just left.

JJ. No, that must be Rod. Rod's been here every day.

ERNIE. You're...what?

JJ. Toto.

ERNIE. That useless piece of shit has abandoned me. Left me on this floor. He's trying to kill me. If he comes back now, I'll have a heart attack when I see him!

JJ. Okay.

ERNIE. Don't let him kill me, JJ, ha? He always wanted me dead. I embarrass him. Not like you.

JJ. I don't know if \ that's how –

ERNIE. I'll have a heart attack, if I see him! Tell him to never come back.

JJ. No, I... I won't tell him that.

ERNIE. You have to!

JJ. But if I tell him coming here will give you another heart attack, and he wants to kill you, then he'll just show up. So I won't tell him, okay? And he won't come.

ERNIE. He won't?

JJ. No. So he can't kill you.

ERNIE. Okay... Don't let him kill me.

JJ. I won't.

ERNIE. You're a good son, JJ. Who needs him? You're a good, good son.

(The compliment hits JJ *like a punch in the gut.)*

JJ. I'm the one who hasn't been here.

ERNIE. I know you're busy. My Hollywood hotshot, ha?

(JJ is silent.)

ERNIE. *(Cont.)* Sit with me. We can play blackjack.

  (JJ doesn't move.)

JJ, come sit.

  (Nothing.)

JJ...?

JJ. Yeah?

ERNIE. Come sit with me. You don't have to do anything. Just sit.

  (JJ doesn't move.)

JJ?

JJ. ...No.

ERNIE. Sit here.

JJ. I'm going to stay here. No. I'm going to stand here.

ERNIE. Why?

JJ. I just am.

ERNIE. Okay.

JJ. Actually, I'm going to go.

ERNIE. Okay. I'll see you tomorrow.

JJ. No.

ERNIE. So busy. Soon you'll be famous. I'll see you on the television, right? Your movie.

JJ. No, I mean, this is the last time you're going to see me. This is goodbye.

ERNIE. JJ...?

JJ. Toto loves you. I'm the one who...

When I got back, everything was a disaster. But you were millimeters from dying, so I set it all aside and prepared myself.

And then you got better. Not one hundred percent, but enough. And I wished – I wished...

Toto made all the right decisions, and you're here now, because of him.

I haven't visited you, Dad. For weeks.

I was afraid to come, because I need help, and now I
see you, and I know: you could never help me. You hate
the world. And I can't anymore. I need to live in it.

I'm leaving. I'm starting over.

Look at you.

>*(Ten seconds.)*

ERNIE. Good-bye.

JJ. Good-bye.

>*(JJ turns.)*

ERNIE. YOU'RE KILLING ME!

>*(JJ stops.)*

I'm having a heart attack. YOU'RE BREAKING MY
HEART – YOU'RE KILLING ME!

>*(JJ turns back to him and charges right up to the
side of the bed.)*

JJ. No one is killing you! You're dying like everyone dies.
Blaming everyone won't make you any less terrified.
You'll just be alone.

People all around you want to help you, if you let them
instead of accusing them of murder.

ERNIE. Okay, then help me. Please, JJ, sit here and help
me.

>*(Ten seconds.)*

JJ. I'll get Toto. He'll be here soon.

>*(JJ exits into the hallway, as **ERNIE** reaches out for
him.)*

>*(**TWEE** is in the hall waiting.)*

TWEE. You did it.

JJ. Yeah.

>*(Five seconds.)*

Twee…

TWEE. So what now?

JJ. I'm going home. To LA.

TWEE. One visit and then mic drop?

JJ. Yes.

TWEE. I rescind my previous statement and once again wish I had a set like yours.

JJ. You do.

TWEE. No

  …

  No.

  …

  …

  I just. I just stood there.

  Everyone was running around, and I just stood there.

  And you can't really say, "Fuck 'em all," because they're trying to help. Mo helped. She actually fit. I don't really know if she's as good as people say, but she looked amazing.

  And usually I'm the one…she just stands there, and I'm amazing…right?

  Just not when it would have counted.

  My precious mother is dead, and I just stood there.

>   (JJ *holds her.*)

JJ. I'm sorry. Your mother was special.

TWEE. She slapped you.

JJ. I deserved it.

TWEE. You're leaving.

JJ. I'll stay for her service. I'll stay awhile.

TWEE. And then…

JJ. I'll go home.

TWEE. What'll I do?

JJ. I don't know.

TWEE. I don't know.

  What'll I do?

  I really don't know.

(They hear **ERNIE** *moan from within the room. Then…)*

ERNIE. My heart is breaking! You leave me? I'LL LEAVE YOU! I'll be gone, and then what? WHAT WILL YOU DO?

End of Scene

Scene Twelve

(The next morning at the hospital. **HENRY** *stands outside of Room 722 as* **ROD** *enters.)*

ROD. Is he up?

HENRY. I think so. You should ask Dr. Tyrone how he is.

ROD. But you know how he's doing, right? You've been here.

HENRY. Yes. He's in a lot of pain again. They still don't know what the infection keeping him here is, but it's not responding to any antibiotics. He might have to go back to the ICU. They've increased his painkillers. He's not all there today.

ROD. Thanks.

HENRY. How's Momo?

ROD. She's gone home, finally. I'm just checking on him and then heading out myself. You?

HENRY. Done here. So…just going home. I guess.

ROD. Good.

HENRY. Good.

ROD. Okay… I'm going to check on my dad.

HENRY. Okay. Maybe… I'll wait? In case you need anything.

ROD. Like what…?

HENRY. I don't know. In case you need anything.

(ROD doesn't know what to say, so he says nothing. He goes into the room.)

(ERNIE lays in the bed as before. He's much more drugged up and gazes around the room with a glassy, opiate stare. He holds the deck of cards in one hand.)

ROD. How's it going today?

(ERNIE reaches out his hand. **ROD** *isn't sure what to do, but he eventually takes it.* **ERNIE** *pulls him closer.)*

ERNIE. My son…my son is a useless piece of shit.

ROD. Yeah.

(**ERNIE** *releases his hand.*)

Your other son was here.

ERNIE. He can't move me to the other floor.

ROD. You may get back there all on your own. You must have been happy to see JJ.

ERNIE. I don't need him. I need the useless piece of shit to move me to the other floor.

ROD. He's trying. To help. He's here every day.

ERNIE. I need him. And he needs me. JJ doesn't need me. JJ is smart. Like me.

ROD. Why does…your other son need you?

ERNIE. JJ knows I'm shit. Toto is weak.

(**ROD** *stares at his father.*)

Toto forgives me.

(**ROD** *starts to leave the room. He can't.*)

ROD. Why does he forgive you?

ERNIE. I don't know. My father was a cruel man. He locked us in the outhouse when we misbehaved. He left me there overnight once, bitten by flies and mosquitos. He beat us just for opening our mouths. No one told me how to be a father, so I didn't try. If I leave them alone, I can't mess up. They'll go on without me. But I did mess up. And JJ will never forgive me. Good. He'll be okay when I go. He'll go on.

ROD. But Rod…Toto?

ERNIE. Toto thinks one day I'll be a good dad. I'll never be a good dad. But Toto forgives. He needs to come here and see me for what I am.

ROD. I think he does, but he forgives you anyway.

ERNIE. He has to stop letting people get away with shit. Tell them to fuck off and leave him alone. Be strong like me. Then he'll have a good life. Like me.

ROD. A good life. Like yours?

ERNIE. Yes.

ROD. If he tells people to fuck off and stops letting them get away with shit, he'll have a life just like yours.

ERNIE. Yes.

>*(A beat.)*

ROD. Are you comfortable?

ERNIE. Yes.

ROD. I'll check on you tomorrow. And your son will see you then, okay? Tomorrow.

>*(**ROD** exits the room and sees **HENRY** still waiting outside the door.)*

You…you're still here.

HENRY. I'm still here.

>*(**ROD** walks past him to go.)*

At least let me…let me buy you dinner. A regular dinner. You're not eating again.

ROD. Henry…

HENRY. Please. I thought it would be too hard. But this is harder.

Be angry. Don't forgive me. Just…dinner. I'll wear a really, really ugly shirt.

I can do that, Rod. Let me.

ROD. Okay. I will. Thank you.

>*(**HENRY** puts his arm over **ROD**'s shoulder as they exit.)*

End of Scene

Scene Thirteen

(MOMO sitting in VERA*'s living room with her laptop.)*

MOMO. Ang babae at ang kanyang kabayo. [A woman and her horse.]

(TWEE enters.)

Kumakain sila ng kanilang mga mansanas. [They eat their apples.]

(MOMO sees her and takes off the headphones.)

TWEE. I didn't hear you come in. Dad should have woken me.

MOMO. He didn't want to. You were up all night. So I thought I'd just... I'd do this.

TWEE. Everything at the hospital...?

MOMO. Is taken care of.

TWEE. Dad wants us to go through everything before her sisters come. Where is he?

MOMO. *(Gesturing over her shoulder.)* He's in the TV room. I'll get him.

TWEE. No. He did so much yesterday. I'm actually glad he stopped for a minute.

MOMO. Okay. Well... I'm almost finished with this lesson.

TWEE. Yeah. Okay.

(MOMO puts on the headphones. TWEE looks over her shoulder.)

MOMO. Ang mga magulang at ang kanilang mga anak na babae. [Parents and their daughters.]

(TWEE sits next to her.)

Ang batang lalaki at ang kanyang tatay. [A boy and his father.]

(MOMO notices TWEE looking. She lowers the headphones and repositions the laptop, so TWEE can get a better view. She points to the screen.)

MOMO. *(Cont.)* Ito ang pamilya ko. "This is my family."

> *(*TWEE *stares at her.)*

Ito ang pamilya ko.

TWEE. Ito ang...

MOMO. Pamilya. Just like "family."

TWEE. Ito ang pamilya ko.

MOMO. Oo. Magaling. [Yes. Good.]

Ito ang tatay ko. [This is my father.]

> *(*TWEE *points to the TV room.)*

TWEE. Ito ang tatay ko.

MOMO. Oo.

(Pointing to the screen.) Ito ang nanay ko. [This is my mother.]

> *(Pause.)*

TWEE. Hindi. Hindi ang nanay. [No. No mother.]

> *(*TWEE *tears up. She starts falling apart.)*

MOMO. Hindi.

(Points to the screen.) Ito ang kapatid kong babae. [This is my sister.]

> *(*TWEE *is silent.)*

(Pointing to TWEE.*)* Ito ang kapatid kong babae. "My sister."

TWEE. Ito ang...ito ang kapatid...kong babae.

MOMO. Magaling.

> *(*TWEE *slams the laptop shut. She's crying now.* **MOMO** *might be crying, too.)*

TWEE. How can you...? I DON'T KNOW WHAT I'M DOING, MOMO. And you just –

MOMO. You made me strong.

TWEE. Without her to take care of me, what am I going to do?

MOMO. *(Pointing to herself.)* Ito ang iyong kapatid na babae. [This is your sister.]

TWEE. FUCK OFF!

> (**MOMO** *takes* **TWEE**'s *hand and presses it to her.*)

MOMO. ITO ANG KAPATID KONG BABAE.

TWEE. *(Understanding.)* Ito…ito ang kapatid kong babae. Oo.

MOMO. Magaling.

TWEE. Salamat. [Thanks.]

MOMO. You're welcome.

> (**MOMO** *and* **TWEE** *mourn together.*)
>
> *(Lights shift.)*
>
> (**ERNIE** *gazes into the audience with a glassy stare. As a warped and trippy version of the opening hymn fills the air, he smiles at a good-looking woman. His grip loosens on the cards. They slip out of his hand and onto the floor.)*

End of Scene

End of Play